Everything is OK

PAULA VI

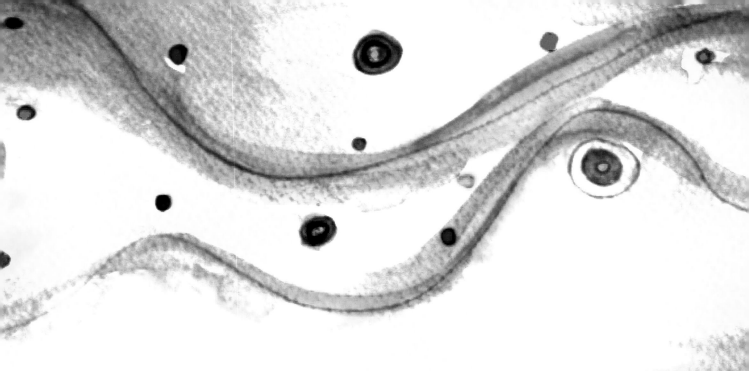

For my children,

Candice, Cassie, Brooke, Jacquiline, Thomas

and my grandchildren

Oscar, Miah and Connor

and the child within all of us.

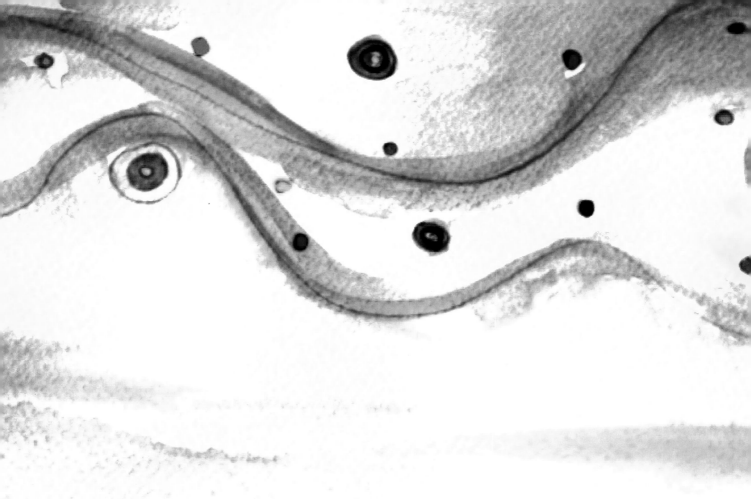

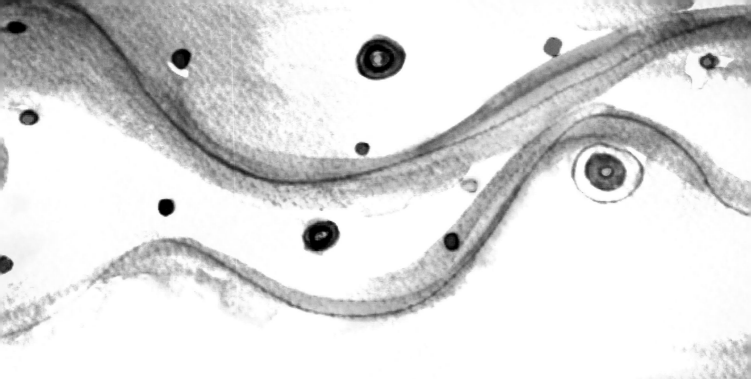

Everything is OK

The sun was bright and Oscar Kahn could feel the warmth on his face.
He jumped up out of bed, his cape flying up in the air as he ran down the hallway to where his Mum was.
"Good morning Oscar," she said.
"Good morning Mum," he replied before turning to smile at his younger brother Connor.
Connor smiled right back at him. Oscar, excited, yelled out;
"Mum can we go swimming?"
"Yes Oscar of course we can, two things before we do."
"What Mum?" he asked, not sure exactly what she was thinking.
"Well Oscar the first thing is your manners, let's say the manners poem that your great grandmother used to recite to your Nanna."
"Ok," Oscar replied.

It goes like this: "Thank you and please are two little keys that open and shut every door, and if you use them you are bound to get a whole lot more."

"Sorry I forgot to use my manners Mum, but what is the second thing?" he asked.

"Your dreaming Oscar, Connor and I want to hear all about your dreaming," she said.

Oscar moved and sat next to his Mum and Connor to tell of his dreaming as "Captain OK".

Oscar started telling of his dreaming as "Captain OK."

"Josh the Dragon came and we flew to the Dreaming Land"

"When we arrived, Noah the Crystal Man was there with Finn the Meditator who was showing Noah how to meditate by using all your Chakra points and your Breath," he continued.
"All the Fairies and Miah were there too."
Miah is a cousin of Oscar's; or Captain OK as he is known in the Dreaming.
She has a direct connection to the moon. Miah was born on a full blue moon in the year 2012 and she also is connected to all the orbs that travel the universe at night.

After Noah had done some meditating, he showed the fairies how to get the healing powers from the crystals.

He had made mandalas from the crystals to connect with the universe and its amazing powers.

Mandalas are an ancient art of circles that tell stories from many lives ago. Noah has a lot of ancient memories because his soul has travelled and had many lives.

Jacqueline the Fire Fairy was laughing because Alectro the
Wizard kept moving the crystals around. Noah started
laughing too.
All of this joy and happiness made all the other fairies laugh
and dance. Mieke the Water Fairy grabbed the hand of the
head fairy.
The head of the fairies name was never spoken in the
Dreaming and normally no one would touch her, but Mieke
always did what she wanted as a rule. So they danced and
laughed along with everyone else and this made glitter rain
from the sky.

They were having so much fun so Captain OK and Josh the Dragon left. They went to the lake to visit Caitlin the Mermaid Princess. Josh likes to visit her and play his viola while Caitlin swims around, splashing and dancing to the beautiful sound. When they arrived Caleb the Water Serpent was sitting on a rock and looking a little sad. "What's wrong?" asked Josh. "Caitlin is angry with me," replied Caleb.
"Why is Caitlin angry with you?" both Josh and Captain OK asked. "Well I was only joking and said that I didn't believe she could do magic," Caleb said.
Josh and Captain OK decided to speak to Caitlin about what Caleb had said.

"Caitlin, Caitlin!" they yelled. Within a few minutes she swam to the shore and then flew up around them, splashing all the three boys with water.

She was beautiful. Her blue fairy wings and her aqua blue tail sparkled under the stars.

"Why are you boys yelling at me?" she asked.

"We heard that Caleb had made you feel upset," said Josh.

"Well first of all boys remember nobody can make me feel anything, my feelings are my choice," she said.

"I am in control of them and nobody else is in control of how I feel.

But yes, I did feel a bit upset."

Before Caitlin could finish Ty appeared. Usually Ty is bright and very white in her karate GI. But instead, she was all muddy and dull.

"Hurry, hurry. Captain OK, there is trouble in the Valley of Shadows," Ty said.

"Miah, Kayla and Charlie where flying through the valley and the dark spirit has tried to take their light."

Charlie and Kayla are the youngest of the fairies and Miah is only two years old. They loved playing together.

Charlie is so bright and pink all over,
except for her face.
She is very gifted and she
is a healing pixie.
Kayla is always flying in circles
and throwing pink Fairy dust
over everyone.
They were flying and lost their
way and they had forgotten
their protection before
they went dreaming.

Captain OK summoned Zak the Purple Dragon.
By now everyone had heard the call. This time they didn't yell, they used the gift of mind speaking and the reading of peoples thought. because they were all in the 5th Dimension, which everyone can be when you are in your dreaming, they could all hear and speak to each other without actually saying a word.
This is called telepathy.
Even Alectro the Wizard, who was always travelling to different countries in his dreaming, heard the call.

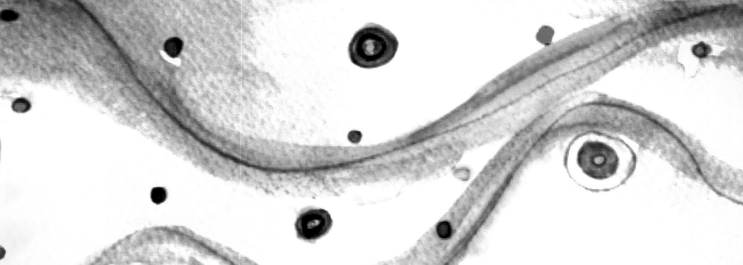

Ty got on Zak's back and headed towards the Valley of Shadows.

Captain OK arrived at the same time. He knew how to travel by time portals in the Universe; another of his gifts.

Caitlin and Caleb were on the back of Josh the dragon, and he was very fast and knew the area well.

Captain OK swooped in and told them to follow him. They all went high above the Valley of Shadows so they could see what was going on beneath them.
Josh used his astro vision to look through the trees and see what was going on.
He could see Charlie, Kayla and Mian sitting on a large rock and they looked a little bit scared.

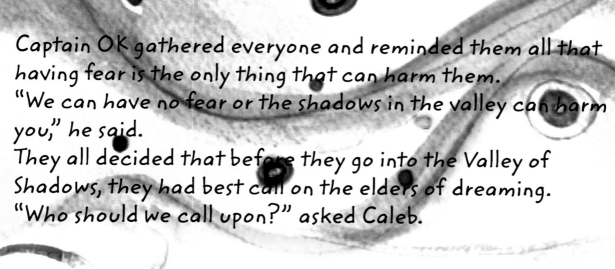

Captain OK gathered everyone and reminded them all that having fear is the only thing that can harm them.
"We can have no fear or the shadows in the valley can harm you," he said.
They all decided that before they go into the Valley of Shadows, they had best call on the elders of dreaming.
"Who should we call upon?" asked Caleb.

Captain OK suggested Tom, who is an Aboriginal elder in the country of Australia, he is captain OK's Nannas spirit guide, well one of them.
Then Noah suggested Captain OK and Miah's Nanna. They all decided that Tom was the best choice because spirit guides are very powerful in the Dreaming.
Before they had even finished the sentence, Tom appeared. He was tall and strong with the biggest happiest smile you have ever seen. But he was also wise and can sometimes look a bit scary, at least some of the fairies think so anyway.

"Hello everyone," said Tom. "What's happening, why have I been summoned?"

Josh explained that Charlie, Kayla and Miah had flown into the Valley of the Shadows while they were playing and didn't have their protection.

"We saw them in there and they looked a bit scared," he added.

Tom said exactly what Oscar had told the group about fear.

"Have no fear and you will be OK. But I will also watch over you," he said.

"Can you remember what the two strongest protections against fear and negativity are?"

"I know," said Michael the white knight.

Michael was a knight in the Dreaming and Bravery is his gift, he rides a large white Unicorn. Tom handed him the speaking stick, an old ancient stick used so that when you are handed it everyone must be quiet and listen to the person who holds it.

"It's joy and happiness," Zak said with excitement.
"That's exactly right," replied Tom, showing extreme pride at how Michael had been such a good speaker and listener. He developed this from the weekly classes that Tania and Captain OK's Nanna taught.
"So how do we do that?" asked Ty.
"Do we karate chop them?"
"No," replied Tom. "You simply laugh and the entire negative energy will leave, you can't have fear when you have joy and you can't have sadness when you have happiness."

"That's right!" shouted Oscar.
"Remember Caitlin before when you were angry and you splashed us and we laughed, everything was much happier and positive."
"That's true," replied Caitlin, who said the vibration from that positive energy made them all laugh.
Everyone started laughing just at the thought of Caitlin splashing the boys with water.
"There you go, you are all now ready to go into the Valley of Shadows," Tom said.
"Remember if fear comes, just laugh at it."

They all started laughing and singing as they flew into the
Valley of Shadows.
"There they are," whispered Captain OK.
Everyone landed and sat down next to Charlie, Kayla and
Miah.
"What happened that made you so scared," asked Jacqueline
and Mieke, at the exact same time. They are twins and
sometimes speak in unison.
Kayla explained that while they were in their dreaming, a dark
entity called Zar appeared he was trying to scare them by
saying that happiness and joy were not real and that sadness
and fear were what they should believe in.

"His voice was so scary and deep and he is an adult, we are just children, aren't we meant to believe what adults say?" Kayla said. "Then he took Miah's orbs and said that our magic powers and the dreaming are not real either. He even said that Fairies do not exist." "No, No!" said the group. "That's a misbelief, adults can lose their dreaming, but that doesn't mean it isn't real," explained Mistogen. Mistogen is an element of the universe. In the dreaming he appears a wind, fog or mist and when he speaks it is felt more the

He is the cousin of Hannah the Seer, who can look into the future and has been taught and protected by Miah and Captain OK's Nanna.

She has a sister Brooke, who is a beautiful Irish princess in the dreaming and has the gifts of joy and humour.

Brooke is one of the funniest people you will ever meet.

Hannah and Mistogen are good friends as well as family.

Their other good friend is Nicola she is the Dragon of Knowledge.

Nicola is Alectro's older sister.
Nicola was devastated that Zar had tried to use such scary tactics on the younger children.
She explained that most humans exist in the 4th dimensional space and that dreaming is in the higher 5th dimensional space, the same space as where people go when they meditate.
All the children were now sitting in a circle and listening to the older ones speaking through their knowledge and wisdom.
Mistogen explained that most of humanity has fear and society puts boundaries on people to create fear-based responses. "This limits our imagination," he said.

Nicola interrupted and explained that as children we hear easier and we understand the words that Mistogen uses, easier than when we are older.

Mistogen, Hannah, Brooke and Nicole or as the younger ones like to call them, the Amazing Four, often spoke in the higher 5th dimensional space. The vibration there is very high as they are all teenages now.

The universe is made from vibrations. We all hear it differently depending on where our vibrational energy sits.

"No one is lesser or more,
we are all in the place we
should be, where our soul's
journey is," explained Hannah.

"Let me explain it a little easier," said Brooke.
"Every choice we make is either positive or negative. Negative is fear and that is a low vibration.
"Positive is happiness and joy and it is a very high vibrational energy."
"I see the future," said Hannah.
"If you could see what I see, then you would know that a life filled with fear and negativity is not a good life to live for any soul."
"Tell us more about the future," the children asked.
"No I can't, and won't ever speak your future because the one thing about the future is what
I see in your future today you
can change tomorrow as
you lift your vibrational
energy higher and higher into
your 5th dimension."

Just then Tom appeared and explained
that every day we make choices.
"Sometimes you may make negative
choices and not do as your Mum,
Dad or carer asks you too," he said.
"We all choose negatively sometimes,
but you control your behaviour
and choices every day of your life.

"Remember also to dream is a gift. Never stop dreaming and imagining what you would like your life and future to be."
All the children cheered. At that moment the sun rose up through the night sky.
"My dreaming ended then Mum," Oscar said.
"I can't wait to go to bed tonight to have more dreaming. Can we go swimming now please?"
"Of course Oscar, go and put your swimmers on while I get Connor ready," she said.
He gave his Mum a big hug and thanked her for believing in his dreaming.

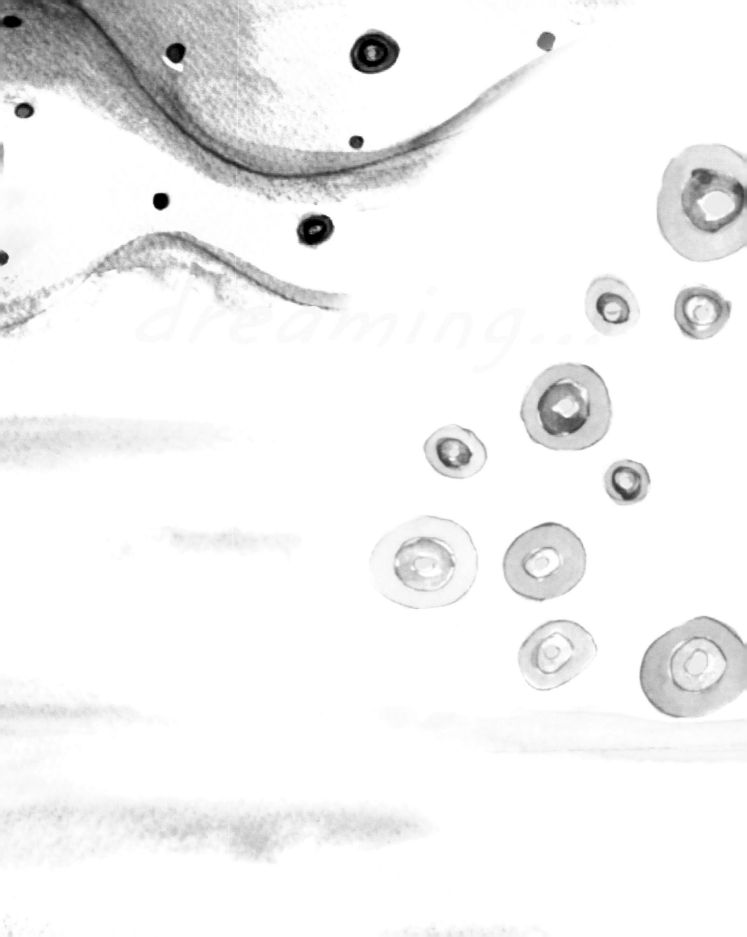

Meanings

Mandalas ~ ancient circles representing stories

Ancient Memories ~ memories from past lives that your soul has travelled

4th Dimension ~ Human beings with good intent

5th Dimension ~ State of dreaming and meditation

Fairies ~ Often small in size and are seen in the 5th dimensional space

Wizard ~ A person with a gift of powers and knowledge to create spells

Viola ~ large stringed instrument that has a deep sound

Mermaid Princess ~ a beautiful being that can swim and fly

Spirit Guides ~ A soul that has not past over and has chosen to guide gifted people with knowledge and understanding also protects the humans they are guiding

Water Serpent ~ a snake like being that is very wise

Telepathy ~ the gift of reading minds without using words from your mouth but through thought

Time Portals ~ a space within the Quantum universal dimension that enables travel

Quantum ~ the universal dimension

Meataphysics ~ Human dimension

Astro ~ Vison or travelling with and outer body experience

Speaking Stick ~ An ancient stick that is used for speaking in higher self

Unison ~ doing something at the exact same time

Element of the Universe ~ is not a person or a spirit it is Wind, Earth, Water or fire

Seer ~ the gift of seeing spirits, ghosts and 5th dimensional beings

Knowledge ~ information that is held in the subsconscious mind

Chakra ~ points of energy within your body

"The meanings listed above are my knowledge and truth".

- Paula Vi

I would like to show gratitude and thanks to

I want to thank my Mum, Dixie, for always telling me that everything about me was perfect.

My brother Geoff, for raising me from the age of 9, without you I would not be the woman I am today.

To my dear friend Barb and her Mum Dorothy for all your love and support you have given to me.

To the children who are the characters in the book and your parents for allowing me the honour to have you my classes each week.

To all my friends for your constant support and kindness, my love and gratitude always.

To my dear friend and collegue Tania Davies for all your support, knowledge, caring and belief in energy and the children.

To the 5 souls that chose me as your Mum, thank you for the journey and to my grandchildren to whom my soul will always be connected.

Gratitude Always

Paula Vi

Lightning Source UK Ltd.
Milton Keynes UK
UKRC02n2240010818
326647UK00007B/98